FAVORITE CAT BREEDS

RAGDOLL CATS

by Mari Schuh

AMICUS HIGH INTEREST • AMICUS INK

Amicus High Interest and Amicus Ink are imprints of Amicus
P.O. Box 227, Mankato, MN 56002
www.amicuspublishing.us

Library of Congress Cataloging-in-Publication Data
Schuh, Mari C., 1975- author.
Ragdoll cats / by Mari Schuh.
pages cm. -- (Favorite cat breeds)
Audience: K to grade 3.
Summary: "A photo-illustrated book for early readers about Ragdoll cats. Describes the Ragdoll's unique features, large size, flu ff yc oat, social behaviors, and how they act as pets"-- Provided by publisher.
Includes bibliographical references and index.
ISBN 978-1-60753-971-1 (library binding)
ISBN 978-1-68152-100-8 (pbk.)
ISBN 978-1-68151-005-7 (ebook)
1. Ragdoll cat--Juvenile literature. 2. Cat breeds--Juvenile literature. I. Title.
SF449.R34S38 2017
636.8'3--dc23
2015028771

Photo credits: Eric Isselee/Shutterstock cover; Susan Schmitz/Shutterstock 2; Jane Burton/Dorling Kindersley Ltd./Corbis 5; Tony Campbell/Shutterstock 6-7; petfoto/Alamy 9; Gary Ombler/Dorling Kindersley Ltd./Corbis 10-11; Juniors/Juniors169003/Superstock 13, 17; O.DIGOIT/Alamy 14-15; Juniors Bildarchiv GmbH/Alamy 18-19; beinder/iStock 20-21; Jean-Michel Labat/ardea.com/Pantheon10775491/Superstock 22

Editor: Wendy Dieker
Designer: Tracy Myers
Photo Researcher: Rebecca Bernin

For Liz and Rich—MS

TABLE OF CONTENTS

BIG AND FLUFFY

A big cat follows its owner. It walks from room to room. The fluffy cat has blue eyes. Its tail is bushy. It is a Ragdoll.

Fun Fact
Ragdolls are called "puppy cats." They follow their owners like a puppy.

HISTORY

Ragdolls came from California. A breeder named Ann Baker started the **breed**. In the 1960s, she bred cats with long hair. The cats were quiet. They were gentle.

Fun Fact

Ragdolls got their name from how they act. They flop like a child's rag doll when they are picked up.

LONG, HEAVY CATS

Ragdolls are big and heavy. They have long bodies. They are one of the heaviest cat breeds. Males can weigh 20 pounds (9 kg).

Like a Wild Cat?

Bobcats are the smallest wild cats. They are only a little bit bigger than the largest Ragdoll cats.

MANY COLORS AND PATTERNS

Ragdolls can be many colors and patterns. Many Ragdoll **coats** are a light color. Ragdolls often have darker fur on their faces, ears, legs, and tails.

SOFT AND SILKY

Ragdolls have medium-long fur. It is soft and silky. It feels like rabbit fur. Ragdolls have long fur around their necks. It is called a **ruff**.

Like a Wild Cat?

A Ragdoll's ruff is much like a lion's mane. This fur covers its head and neck.

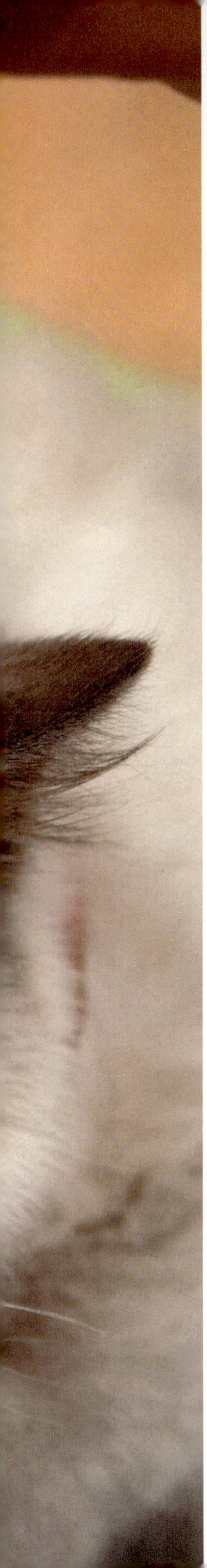

GROOMING

A Ragdoll is easy to **groom**. Its fur rarely gets **matted**. These cats need to be combed at least once a week.

KITTENS

Mother Ragdolls have about five kittens at a time. The kittens are born white. Their full coat color grows in after about two years. By age 4, they are fully grown.

SWEET, LOVING CATS

Ragdolls are sweet and polite. They are loving, playful pets. Ragdolls let kids dress them up in doll clothes. These cats also play fetch.

CALM AND EASYGOING

Ragdolls are quiet and easygoing. They are calm, relaxed cats. Ragdolls let people hold them like a baby. They are great family pets.

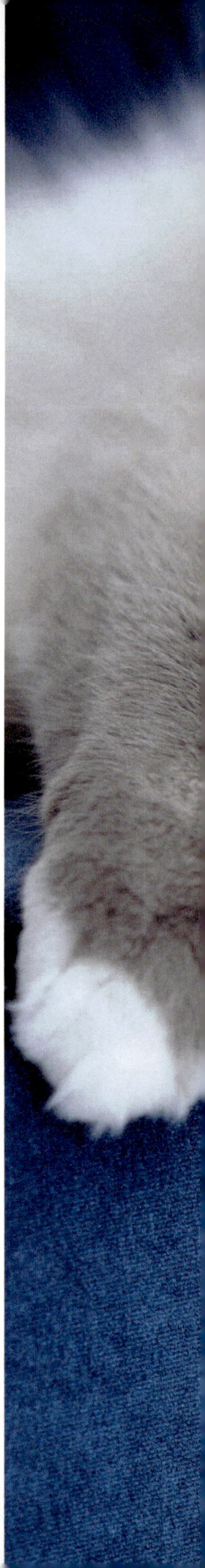

HOW DO YOU KNOW IT'S A RAGDOLL?

WORDS TO KNOW

breed – a type of cat

coat – an animal's hair or fur

groom – to comb or brush; to clean and take care of

matted – when fur turns into a thick, tangled lump

ruff – a ring of long hair around a cat's neck

LEARN MORE

Books

Felix, Rebecca. *Ragdolls.* Cool Cats. Minneapolis: Bellwether Media, 2016.

Holland, Gini. *Ragdolls.* Cats Are Cool. New York: PowerKids Press, 2014.

Websites

Cat Fanciers' Association: For Kids
http://kids.cfa.org/index.html

Discovery Kids: Top Cats
http://discoverykids.com/articles/top-cats/

INDEX

Every effort has been made to ensure that these websites are appropriate for children. However, because of the nature of the Internet, it is impossible to guarantee that these sites will remain active indefinitely or that their contents will not be altered.